Sarah Edmonds

Sunshine PIE

This book belongs to

....

In memory of lovely Jen, a true ray
of sunshine on every adventure. — SE

Published in 2023 by Welbeck Flame
An imprint of Welbeck Children's Limited,
part of the Welbeck Publishing Group
Offices in: London - 20 Mortimer Street, London W1T 3JW
Sydney - 205 Commonwealth Street, Surry Hills 2010
www.welbeckpublishing.com

Senior Editor: Jenni Lazell
Design Manager: Matt Drew

A CIP catalogue record for this book is available from the British Library.

978-1-8013-0107-7

Printed in Heshan, China

9 8 7 6 5 4 3 2 1

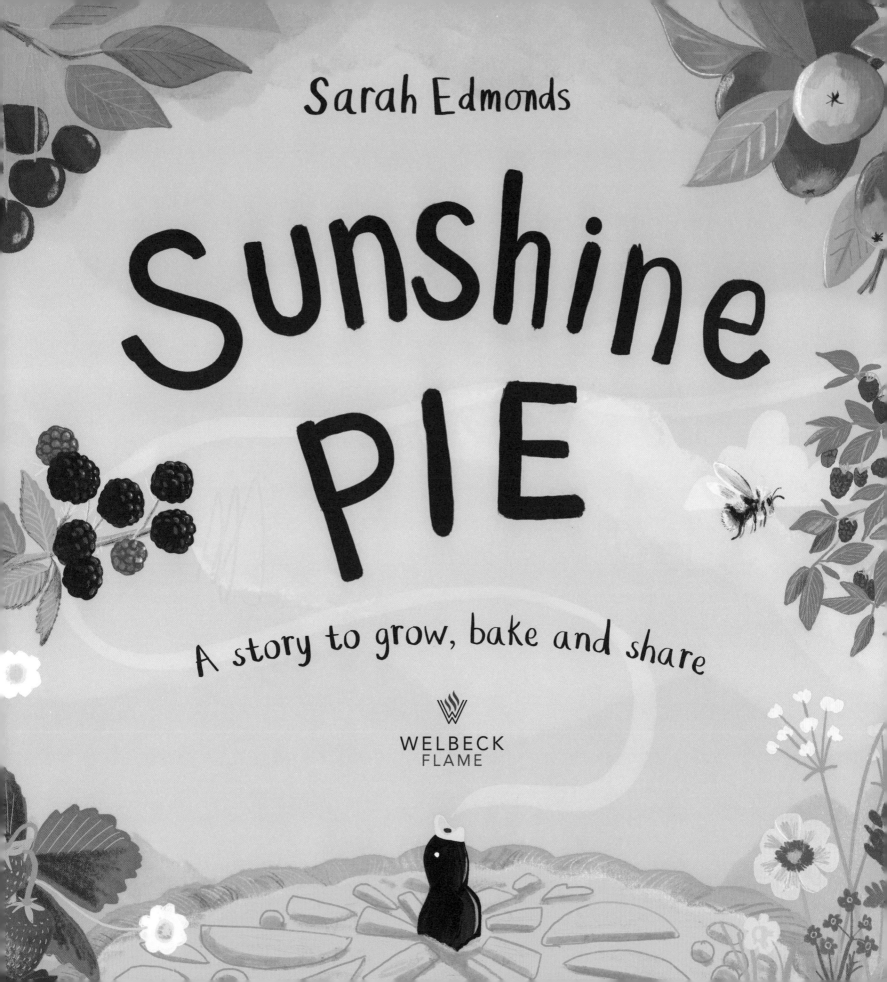

Sarah Edmonds

Sunshine PIE

A story to grow, bake and share

WELBECK
FLAME

Today I'm visiting Aunty Jen. We're having a picnic in the garden. We're making a pie!

"Hello, Olive. We've got lots to do – let's go!"

First we're getting the ingredients for the pie crust...

...and here's the cream for pouring on top.

"This pie is going to be SO big and tasty!"

I ask Aunty Jen, what's going inside our pie?

"SUNSHINE! We're making a sunshine pie."

What's a sunshine pie?

I squint at the sky as we walk along the lane.

How do you catch the sun?

"We're nearly there, Olive. I'll show you..."

We're at the farm!

"See these shiny blackberries? Each and every one has the rays of the sun inside it. That's what makes them so sweet and juicy."

I check the raspberries.
There's definitely
sunshine in these, too.

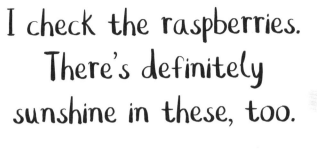

"Aunty Jen — are you
EATING the raspberries?"

"Just testing!"

Now we're picking apples.
They shine and glow
in the sunlight.

I pick the low ones
and Aunty Jen picks
the high ones.

Look at her go!

Aunty Jen's
the BEST.

I help to weigh the fruit.

"Great haul!"

"We're using it ALL in our sunshine pie. Would you like to come to our picnic?"

Our final stop is for free range eggs.

"Freshly laid this morning!" calls Arthur.

Aunty Jen's invited Arthur to the picnic, too.

"If I get the flowers watered then I'll be there. Even better if it rains, it'll save me the trouble."

"Not RAIN! We're having a SUNSHINE pie."

"Come on, Olive, the sky is still bright and we have lots to do. Bye, Arthur!"

Back in the kitchen,
we're making the pie crust.

I rub the butter into
the flour until it's crumbly.

Aunty Jen adds a
little splash of water,

then together
we roll out
the pastry.

Into the bowl goes the sunshine filling. We sprinkle sugar and spices then stir big circles around our dish.

"Remember to make a wish!"

It's pie building time! We line our dish with pastry, pour in our sunshine mix, then cover it with a pastry lid.

This egg looks like sunshine too. We paint our pie to make it golden.

Our sunshine pie is ready to bake...

Into the oven
it goes!

I'm going to find the best picnic spot in the garden.

"Aunty Jen, it's RAINING!"

"Can we still have
our picnic even
though it's raining?"

"Of COURSE we can.
We'll have it in the Kitchen."

"Aunty Jen, is it still a sunshine pie?"

"Of COURSE it is. But it's a rain pie too."

"Inside our pie are the raindrops that
helped the fruit trees grow."

So, it's actually a sunshine-and-rain pie...

The pie is hot and bubbling,
golden and round and ready!

Now the pie is cooling, it's time to set the table.

DONG!

Aunty Jen smiles. "That sounds like someone at the door..."

Our picnic has turned into a PARTY!

And when the pie's all gone, we go out into the garden and see...

A RAINBOW!

Bake your own SUNSHINE pie!

The PASTRY

400g (14 oz) plain flour
200g (7 oz) butter
50g (1.7 oz) caster sugar
1 egg yolk
3 tbsp water

The FILLING

400g (14 oz) blackberries
and raspberries
2-3 large apples (300g / 10.5 oz)
50g (1.7 oz) caster sugar
1 tsp cinnamon
1 egg (for glazing)

Method

1 Preheat your oven to 180°C (350°F) and grease your pie dish with a little butter.

2 First, make the pastry. Rub together the flour and butter until crumbly, then add the sugar. Stir in the egg yolk and a small amount of water and use your hands to bring the mixture together into a dough, adding a little more water if it's too dry. Divide the pastry into two blobs and put them in the fridge for 20 minutes.

3 Wash and weigh the berries and peel, core and cube the apples. Put them in a big mixing bowl along with the sugar and cinnamon. Gently stir it all together – make a wish!

4 Now it's time to build your pie. Roll out one ball of pastry into a circle that's a bit larger than the pie dish and then flop it inside. Press it into the sides and then trim off any extra bits of pastry.

5 Fill your pie dish with the fruity filling, then roll out the other half of your dough to make the pie lid and press it firmly around the edges.

6 Use any leftover pastry to cut out shapes to place on top. Then use a pastry brush to paint your pie with beaten egg.

7 Push the pie bird into the top of the pastry or just add a little hole for the steam. Bake for 30 minutes or until golden.

Your sunshine pie can be eaten hot or cold, come rain or shine.
But the very biggest and best pies are made for SHARING!